MEGAZORD TO THE RESCUE!

By Cathy East Dubowski

A PARACHUTE PRESS BOOK

GROSSET & DUNLAP • NEW YORK

A PARACHUTE PRESS BOOK
Parachute Press, Inc.
156 Fifth Avenue
New York, NY 10010

Published by Grosset & Dunlap, Inc., a member of The Putnam &
Grosset Group, New York. GROSSET & DUNLAP is a trademark of
Grosset & Dunlap, Inc. Published simultaneously in Canada.

Creative Consultant: Cheryl Saban.

With special thanks to Cheryl Saban, Sheila Dennen, Debi Young, and
Sherry Stack.

Printed in the U.S.A.
May 1994
ISBN: 0-448-40830-9
C D E F G H I J

PROLOGUE

The Battle Begins

Long ago, Good and Evil met in a great battle. The wizard Zordon led the forces of Good. He fought against Rita Repulsa, who wanted to rule the universe with her forces of Evil.

Both sides fought hard, but the war ended in a tie. So Zordon and

Rita made a deal. They would both flip coins to decide who was the winner. Whoever made the best three tosses out of five would win. The loser would be locked away forever.

Of course, Zordon did not want to risk the safety of the universe on five coins—unless they were magic coins! So with his five special coins, Zordon won the coin toss. But Rita had one last trick up her sleeve. Before she was locked away, she trapped Zordon in another dimension. Now he must stay inside a column of green light at his command center forever and ever.

Rita and her wicked friends were dropped into an intergalactic prison and flung through space. They crashed into a tiny moon of a faraway planet. After ten thousand years, space travelers found the prison and opened it. Rita and her servants, Baboo, Squatt, Goldar, and Finster, were free!

Rita hadn't changed one bit in ten thousand years. She began planning to take over the universe again. And she saw her first target in the sky above—Earth!

When Zordon heard of Rita's escape, he put his master plan into action. He called Alpha 5, the robot running his command center on Earth. "Teleport to us five of the wildest, most willful humans in the area," he commanded.

"No!" Alpha 5 said. "Not... teenagers!"

But Alpha 5 did as he was told, and teleported five teenagers to the command center.

"Earth is under attack by the evil Rita Repulsa," Zordon explained to the teenagers. "I have chosen you to battle her and save the planet. Each of you will receive great powers drawn from the spirits of the dinosaurs."

Zordon gave each teenager a

belt with a magic coin—a Power Morpher! "When you are in danger, raise your Power Morpher to the sky," Zordon instructed. "Then call out the name of your dinosaur and you will morph into a mighty fighter—a Power Ranger!

"Jason, you will be the Red Ranger, with the power of the great tyrannosaurus," Zordon explained. "Trini will be the Yellow Ranger, with the force of the saber-toothed tiger. Zack will be the Black Ranger, with the power of the mastodon. Kimberly will be the Pink Ranger, with pterodactyl power. And Billy will be the Blue Ranger, backed by the power of the triceratops."

For big problems, the Power Rangers could call upon Dinozords—giant robots they piloted into battle. And if things got really tough, the Dinozords could combine together to make a super-robot—a mighty Megazord!

Power Rangers, dinosaur spirits, and robots—together, these incredible forces would protect the Earth.

But the teenagers had to follow Zordon's three rules:

1. Never use your powers for selfish reasons.

2. Never make a fight worse—unless Rita forces you.

3. Always keep your identities secret. No one must ever find out that you are a Mighty Morphin Power Ranger!

CHAPTER 1

It was Monday morning in Ms. Appleby's science class at Angel Grove High School. Video science projects were due. Near the front of the room, five friends talked about their projects. They looked like ordinary kids.

They weren't. In fact, *they*

would make a good science project themselves—if their classmates only knew!

Jason, Kimberly, Zack, Billy, and Trini had secret powers. Whenever danger threatened the Earth, they changed into the scientifically outrageous Mighty Morphin Power Rangers!

This morning, though, they were just typical students. As the final class bell rang, Ms. Appleby cleared her throat. She folded her hands on her plump middle and smiled. "Good morning, class. I—"

Crash! The classroom door banged open. Two students burst into the room. One was nearly as wide as the door. The other one was skinny and dressed in black. He was holding a camera to his face. They were still filming their video science project!

The skinny kid aimed his camera at the big one and said, "*Bulk, the World's Greatest Guy*, scene 32."

Bulk gave the camera a fake movie-star smile. "I have always enjoyed this wonderful class…"

Their teacher frowned. "Bulk! Skull! Please take your seats."

"That's Ms. Appleby," Bulk said to the camera. "She just can't wait for me to sit down. She really is a lovely teacher."

Bulk backed up to his desk, too busy smiling into the camera to watch where he was going. When he sat down, he missed his chair completely. Books and papers flew everywhere as he crashed to the floor, pulling his desk down on top of him.

Skull recorded it all on camera. Bulk growled at him and shook his fist as he pulled himself up off the floor.

"Don't worry," said Skull. "I'll just cut that part."

Ms. Appleby glared at the two boys, then shook her head and sighed. "Now," she said to the class. "It's time for our video projects. Trini, would you go first, please?"

Tall, willowy Trini walked gracefully to the front of the room. She popped her tape into the VCR, pushed her long black hair over her shoulder, and faced the class. "My video project is called *Pollution Problems in Angel Grove.*"

A close-up of Trini appeared on the TV screen. Her video image said, *"A lot has been done to clean up the environment in the past few years. But pollution is still a problem. Even here in beautiful Angel Grove."*

Trini's classmates stared in surprise at the pictures she had recorded. Scenes of parks littered with soda cans and fast-food wrappers. Factories belching thick black smoke. Lakes choked with grunge and garbage.

Jason shook his head. "This is totally terrible."

Even Zack, who was usually cracking jokes, watched silently.

Trini's face stared back at them from the screen. Her serious dark eyes seemed to look deeply into each viewer's heart as she concluded the video.

"If we destroy nature's delicate balance, the animals will disappear. And if the animals disappear,

we will, too. The time to act is now."

After a moment of silence, the whole class broke into applause.

"Very nice job, Trini," said Ms. Appleby. "Pollution is a serious concern for our society."

"Awesome video!" Kimberly said as Trini took her seat. "What can we do to make things better in Angel Grove?"

"I have an idea," Trini said with an eager smile. "I want to start a Clean-Up Club. Each week we can do some recycling, clean up nature trails, or find ways to save endangered animals."

"Count me in," said Jason.

"Sounds cool," Zack agreed, his dark eyes flashing with excitement.

Full of ideas, the five Power Rangers began to make plans.

Someone was watching them.

Someone who hated them and everything they stood for.

Rita Repulsa muttered as she paced the balcony of her cold, gloomy fortress on the moon. She had dark, cruel eyes and a nasty smile.

Rita giggled wickedly as she spied on the Power Rangers through her powerful telescope. Then she glared at her two warriors, Goldar and Scorpina. "I'll stop their silly cleanup!" she shrieked.

"My new weapon will ruin their whole stupid planet!" said Rita. Then she threw her head back and laughed. "It will make their environment so polluted they'll *never* be able to clean it up!"

CHAPTER 2

Tall, handsome Jason studied his opponent. He calculated space, time, and distance. Then, in one smooth practiced move, he leaped forward.

"Hiii-yaah!"

Jason's hand sliced down on his target.

Crunch!

"Cool," said Zack. "One more aluminum can bites the dust."

Jason's "opponent" was the aluminum soda can he had just flattened. He and Zack were recycling cans at the Angel Grove Youth Center.

"How's it going?" asked Trini. She and the other Power Rangers were wearing their new green Clean-Up Club T-shirts.

"Great," said Zack. He ran his hands through his short, curly dark hair. "Two more cans and we're done."

"Good going, guys," said Trini. Then she joined Billy and

Kimberly across the room. They were helping Ernie, the juice bar owner, set up recycling bins. Billy had used organic paint to label each bin: Glass, Aluminum Cans, and Plastic. He wanted to make sure the bins were organized and efficient.

Kimberly wanted to make sure they looked good! "Okay, a little to the left," she told Ernie.

He moved the bins left.

"Hmm." Kimberly twirled a strand of her shoulder-length brown hair. "Back a little to the right," she said.

Ernie moved the bins right.

"Perfect!"

Trini laughed. "Looks great!"

"No doubt about it," said Zack, as he and Jason joined the others.

Ernie grinned and said, "Hey, you guys, thanks for helping me out with all this recycling stuff."

"No problem," said Trini. "That's what the Clean-Up Club is for." She looked around at her friends. "Are we ready to tackle the field near the park?"

"You bet," said Jason. "Let's go."

As they headed out the door, Bulk and Skull shoved their way in. Bulk was wearing workout clothes. Skull was still shooting the video. "*Bulk, the World's*

Greatest Guy, scene 42."

Bulk smiled at the camera as he headed toward the youth center's exercise machines. "This is where I train. Pumping up is important to me."

"Hey, Bulk," Skull whined. "You promised I could be in this scene with you."

Bulk rolled his eyes. "Who's going to work the camera?" Then Bulk spotted Ernie. "Hey, Ernie, want to film us working out?"

"You guys? Working out?" Ernie tried not to laugh. He'd *never* seen Bulk and Skull working out in the gym before.

Bulk scowled and stuffed the

camera into Ernie's hands. "Just work the camera, okay?"

Ernie shrugged and began to shoot. "Boy, *this* ought to be fun," he said under his breath.

A few blocks away, the Power Rangers came to the field. They couldn't believe what they saw. Old tires, cans, and candy wrappers covered the grass. One of the trash cans had been tipped over, and the wind was scattering its contents across the field.

"This is a mess!" said Trini.

"This is terrible," said Jason.

Trini said, "It's time to take back the field." She held up some extra-large trash bags. "Clean-Up Club to the rescue!"

"Get down," said Zack, high-fiving Jason. Jason, Kimberly, Zack, Trini, and Billy began to clean up—Power Ranger style!

They crisscrossed the field doing back flips and cartwheels, picking up trash as they went.

Zack danced some hip-hop moves across the field. Then he stashed his trash as if he were slam-dunking a basketball into Billy's bag. "Morphinominal!" shouted Zack as he gleefully slam-dunked an apple core.

Working together, they soon had a mountain of trash bags, and the field was almost all clean.

"Looks like our club's really cleaning up," said Jason.

"A very successful venture," Billy agreed, pushing his glasses back up on his nose.

"And it was fun, too," added Zack.

"Now let's do that section over there," said Trini.

The gang jogged off. Moments later Bulk and Skull entered the field and sneaked over to the pile of trash bags.

"This is going to make me look good," Bulk said, his mouth full of banana. "Thanks for all your help, goody-goodies!"

When Bulk finished eating his banana, he just tossed the peel to the ground.

Skull started taping. "Okay, *Bulk, the World's Greatest Guy,* scene 53."

Bulk posed in front of the trash bags. "I picked up all this trash myself," he lied.

"Beautiful, babe," said Skull, stuffing another piece of chewing gum in his mouth. "Now move a little more to the right. No, your right. I mean, *my* right."

Bulk moved left—right—left— and then slipped on the banana peel. *Smoosh!* He landed right in the middle of all the garbage bags.

Trashed by his own litter!

"Skull!" he shouted. "Get me out of here!"

Skull quickly dropped his camera on the grass and grabbed Bulk by the hands. He grunted as he tried to help Bulk up. But Bulk was so heavy he pulled Skull on top of him into the trash instead.

"Good thing nobody can see us," Bulk muttered as they tumbled around in the garbage.

But somebody *was* watching. Actually, some*thing*. The video camera. Skull had forgotten to turn it off.

"I can't wait to send my secret

weapon!" Rita told Goldar as they stood on the balcony of her fortress. "It will destroy the Power Rangers so I can take over the Earth!"

"Another brilliant plan, Your Badness," said Goldar.

"But first," Rita said, "I'll send the Putties to tire out those puny punks!"

Back in the field, the Clean-Up Club was almost finished. Trini wrinkled her nose as she stashed a plate full of rotten food into a bag. "I'm going to put up signs asking people to please use the trash cans."

"Excellent suggestion," said

Billy. "I'll help you."

Suddenly they heard a gurgling sound behind them. Then another. Then more!

"What's that noise?" asked Kimberly. Her brown eyes looked worried.

Billy pointed to the edge of the field. "It's Rita's Putty Patrol!"

"I wonder what Rita's up to this time?" Jason said.

Dozens of the mindless clay fighters began to materialize. Suddenly they surrounded the Power Rangers.

"Aw, man," said Zack. "Now we've got something else to clean up."

"Bag 'em!" Jason cried.

The kids were outnumbered. But they were smarter than the dull-witted Putties.

Zack spun in a circle, knocking six Putties to the ground.

Two Putties rushed Kimberly from both sides. Her dangly gold earrings flashed in the sun as she sprang high above them. Instead of hitting Kimberly, the Putties crashed heads and knocked each other out.

The teens used karate, gymnastic moves, and teamwork to block the Putties' attacks.

Then suddenly, mysteriously, the Putties vanished.

Trini's started a new club—the Clean-Up Club!

Bulk and Skull pretend they want to help with the recycling drive.

The Power Rangers are ready to work hard to clean up the field.

The Putty Patrol stops the cleanup!

Kimberly trashes some Putties!

Pow! Trini's quick moves keep a Putty away.

Trini and Billy enjoy a peaceful moment—now that the Putties are gone!

On the viewing globe, the Power Rangers watch Rita's Polluticorn attack the recycling center.

The air crackles with electricity as the Power Rangers teleport back to Earth.

Trini and Kimberly are ready to morph!

"Need some help, Polluticorn?" asks
Goldar.

Rita's evil warrior gets a Power Ranger punch!

The Power Rangers return to being regular kids—with a big secret!

The kids looked around, gasping for breath. They checked to make sure everyone was okay.

"Trashing those Putties is a big help to our environment," said Zack.

That made everybody laugh. Then a warm breeze carried the scent of flowers toward the Power Rangers. And the birds began to sing again. "It's so peaceful now," said Trini.

"And clean," added Billy.

Just as Kimberly and the others agreed, a horrible roar split the air. The Power Rangers leapt to their feet.

"What's that?" cried Trini.

The Power Rangers looked up. They had never seen anything like the monster hurtling across the sky.

It stood upright like a huge man. But instead of a human head it had the face of a horse and a long black mane. Its body was covered with gray armorlike skin. From the center of its head grew a white horn.

The monster flew on powerful wings—straight toward the Power Rangers!

"Yo, monster horse, sky-high!" Zack said.

"And it's flying in fast!" cried Trini.

"That's one real night-mare," said Kimberly.

Jason knew it would take more than a few karate kicks to stop this monster. "It's morphin time!" he shouted to his friends.

The air crackled with electricity as they raised their Power Morphers to the sky. Just as Zordon had taught them, they called upon the spirits of the ancient dinosaurs.

"Mastodon!" cried Zack.

"Pterodactyl!" cried Kimberly.

"Triceratops!" cried Billy.

"Saber-toothed Tiger!" cried Trini.

"Tyrannosaurus!" cried Jason.

In a flash, the five morphed into—Power Rangers!

Now they stood dressed in shining helmets and sleek jumpsuits; five powerful protectors. Jason the Red Ranger. Kimberly the Pink Ranger. Zack the Black Ranger. Trini the Yellow Ranger. And Billy the Blue Ranger.

The Power Rangers locked hands, uniting their strength. Then together they faced their new foe.

With an unearthly roar, the horse monster flew right at them, knocking them all to the ground.

Dazed, Jason and Zack pulled themselves to their knees.

"Let's get him!" cried Jason.

They ran toward the monster. It just opened its jaws and let out a hideous laugh. Then it blasted them with its magic horn. They were slammed to the ground in a shower of sparks.

Before they could recover, the horse began to flap its huge scary wings. "Power wings, blow!" it roared.

The wind it created was as strong as a tornado. It tossed Zack and Jason through the air like paper dolls. They landed in a red and black heap.

The other Power Rangers rushed to their side. "Are you

guys okay?" Trini asked as she helped them up.

"Come on," said Kimberly. "We've got to stop this thing."

The Power Rangers charged the monster again and again. But nothing worked.

"It doesn't even feel our attacks!" Billy cried.

Lightning flashed from its glowing horn. "I am the Polluticorn," the beast cried, "and I will destroy you and your miserable planet!"

CHAPTER 4

The Polluticorn struck. But the Power Rangers were gone.

Five balls of sparkling colored light, one red, one pink, one black, one yellow, and one blue, streaked across the sky.

They streaked across a distant desert, and were sucked through the roof of a building hidden in the hot sands.

Inside this secret compound, the lights sparkled, and Jason, Trini, Kimberly, Zack, and Billy appeared. They were surrounded by computers and blinking lights.

They were surprised, but not afraid. They had been to this place many times before. This was the command center of Zordon, the good wizard who had given them their powers. He was Rita's age-old enemy. He had pulled them from the battle just in time.

The Power Rangers waited. Soon the image of a pale face

wavered in a column of eerie green light. It almost looked as if it were underwater.

"Zordon," said Jason. "This horse monster is very powerful."

Zordon's image nodded. "It will be difficult to defeat this new monster Rita has created, but not impossible. Billy, please help Alpha 5 with a battle plan while I brief the others."

"Yes, sir," Billy said, and walked over to a small, shiny robot who was fussing over the controls. Red lights blinked around the rim of his metal head.

"So what's the story on this monster, Zordon?" Zack asked.

"It's Rita's latest plan to destroy the Earth," Zordon answered. "Look at the viewing globe."

The Power Rangers gathered around the globe as an image of the winged horse appeared.

"Rita has created the Polluticorn to wipe out the planet with pollution," said Zordon. "His wings create a poison wind. And he fights anything or anyone who tries to clean up pollution."

"There's got to be a way to stop that thing," said Jason.

"But how?" Kimberly asked.

Suddenly they heard Alpha yelping. "Aye-yi-yi-yi-yi!" The little robot had gotten tangled in the computer printouts and was spinning in circles. With a squeak, he crashed to the floor. The Power Rangers ran over to help.

Billy held up the printout and read from it. "My analysis shows that the Polluticorn derives its power from its horn."

Zordon smiled. "Good work, Billy."

Suddenly an alarm sounded. Zordon frowned. "The Polluticorn is attacking the Angel Grove Recycling Center."

The Power Rangers watched on the viewing globe as the building was attacked. Workers scattered as the Polluticorn blasted the recycling center with its horn.

"Ha ha ha! You'll never clean up your pathetic little planet!" the Polluticorn cried.

The Power Rangers' faces were grim as the globe went dark.

"We can't let it wreck the recycling center," said Trini.

"It's morphin time again!" Jason shouted.

The Power Rangers raised their Power Morphers into the air. They called on the powers of the ancient dinosaurs. "Mastodon!" "Pterodactyl!" "Triceratops!" "Saber-toothed Tiger!" "Tyranno-saurus!" A crackling glow filled the command center.

"POWER RANGERS!" the five shouted.

The Power Rangers morphed and began to fade, back to their fight with the Polluticorn.

Zordon's warning echoed after them. "Be careful, Power Rangers. The Polluticorn may not be alone."

CHAPTER 5

Seconds later the Power Rangers materialized at the Angel Grove Recycling Center. With new determination, they faced the Polluticorn.

Just as they were about to charge, Goldar and Scorpina, Rita's two warriors, appeared, blocking their path.

"Need some help, Polluticorn?" Goldar said with a laugh.

"You guys get them," said Jason. "I'll get horn-head!"

Jason charged the Polluticorn. The two enemies struggled hand to hand.

Then Jason was blasted to the ground. He gasped, "I've got to... find a way...to chop off that horn!"

"Face it," the Polluticorn roared. "I'm just too powerful for you, puny Ranger! And your friends are finished. Just like I'm going to finish off this recycling center!"

Jason was back on his feet. "Your polluting days are over, Horseface. I'm sending you back to the barn!"

A cry stopped Jason in his tracks.

"Jason," cried Zack. "Help!" It was a word Zack rarely used. Jason turned and saw that Goldar and Scorpina had knocked the others to the ground. Now they were raising their swords high, about to strike his friends.

"I summon the power of the Dragon Shield!" Jason cried.

Instantly, Jason was covered by a shield of shining gold. The Polluticorn stood between Jason and his friends. Jason faced the Polluticorn, waving his sword bravely.

Again Jason charged. Again the Polluticorn blasted him with its horn. This time, the blows just bounced off the Dragon Shield.

As Goldar and Scorpina watched, Jason sprang as high as he could and raised his sword. Then he swung the blade down with all his might. And the Polluticorn's horn lay smoking on the ground.

The monster grabbed its head. "My horn!" it roared.

Again Jason's sword sliced through the air, this time knocking Goldar and Scorpina's swords to the ground.

High above the Earth, Rita saw the Polluticorn's horn lying in the dirt. "I'll get you for that!" she screamed. She raised her magic staff. She hurled it toward the Earth. "See the Polluticorn grow!"

Rita's staff rocketed to the Earth. The ground shook and lightning flashed, snaking its way to the Polluticorn.

Before the Power Rangers could attack, the monster began to grow. Soon it towered over the tallest buildings in Angel Grove.

"We need Dinozord Power now! Tyrannosaurus!" Jason cried.

"Mastodon!" cried Zack.

"Pterodactyl!" cried Kimberly.

"Triceratops!" cried Billy.

"Saber-toothed Tiger!" cried Trini.

The ground trembled with the distant sound of five dinosaur robots awakening.

Tyrannosaurus erupted from a steaming crack in the ground.

Mastodon broke through its cage of ice.

Triceratops charged across the scorching desert.

Saber-toothed Tiger leaped through a twisted jungle.

Pterodactyl erupted from the fires of a volcano.

Side by side they raced like the wind to answer the call.

The Power Rangers leaped into the air—then landed in the cockpits of their Dinozords.

"Is everybody ready?" Jason shouted.

"Ready!" the Power Rangers cried.

"Okay," said Jason. "Activate Power Crystals...now! Let's show 'em some Megazord Power!"

Two Zords locked into a third, *Clunk! Clang!* and became legs. Two more Zords locked in, *Clang! Thunk!* and formed arms.

The mighty head rose from its chest. Its helmet swung open and locked into place. Its shield clanged into its chest.

In moments the Dinozords had locked together to form a super-robot, the mighty Megazord!

Lights flashed on in the control room behind the Megazord's eyes. All five Power Rangers sat at the controls.

"Come on, guys," said Jason. "Let's round up that horsey!"

The Megazord straightened to its full height. Now the Power Rangers towered over the town of Angel Grove, too.

The Polluticorn flew in for the first strike. The Megazord staggered, but refused to fall.

Then the Polluticorn landed on its clawed feet. It began to flap its huge wings. "Toxic wings, blow!" it cried.

Polluted, hurricane-force winds blew across the landscape. Buildings shook. Huge trees were ripped from the ground. Even the Megazord could not withstand the Polluticorn's power. It tumbled backward through the air.

The ground shook as the Megazord landed. The Power Rangers looked at one another. It was time to call on greater power.

"We need the Power Sword!" Jason cried.

Instantly, a huge sword sliced

toward Earth, the sun glinting off its sharp, shiny blade. It locked into place in the Megazord's powerful hand. Lifting the sword high, the mighty Megazord rose into the air.

The Polluticorn froze. "Huh!? Uh-oh—" It began to back up as the Megazord came toward it.

The Power Sword struck. The Polluticorn was slammed to the ground. In a cloud of crackling electricity and a shower of fireworks and flames, it disappeared.

It was a good day on Earth. The Power Rangers had cleaned up their community. And they had defended the planet from the forces of Evil. Rita Repulsa's particular brand of Evil.

But it was a bad day on the moon—a very bad day. Rita's screams shook the stone walls of her fortress. "Aaaaghh!" she cried as she grabbed the sides of her head. "Those Power Rangers give me a headache!"

CHAPTER 6

Jason, Billy, Trini, Zack, and Kimberly were back in their jeans, T-shirts, and hi-tops, waiting for science class to begin.

Ms. Appleby walked to the front of the room just as the bell rang. She smiled at her students as they took their seats, until her eyes fell on Bulk. Then her smile soured a little. She put her hands on her hips. "Today we'll be seeing Bulk and Skull's video. Won't we?"

Bulk looked over his shoulder. Where is Skull? he thought. "Uh, well, I, uh—"

Crash! The door banged open and Skull rushed into the room. He held up a small black rectangle—the videotape. "Just finished editing it!" he announced.

Ms. Appleby looked doubtful and said, "This should be very interesting."

Bulk smiled nervously. "I'm sure it's an 'A-plus' project." As

Skull sat down, Bulk whispered, "How does it look?"

"A few glitches," Skull said. "But nothing to worry about."

Ms. Appleby started the video. Soon the title appeared on the screen: *Bulk, the World's Greatest Guy*. Bulk grinned conceitedly. A few girls giggled.

Something was wrong, though. Terribly wrong. The tape was all jumpy. The editing was awful. Scenes were mixed up. Sentences were chopped in half.

Bulk began to frown—a big Bulk frown. In the first classroom scene, Bulk seemed to say, *"I...have...no...class."*

"Take your seats," the video Ms. Appleby said.

"That Ms. Appleby...can't... teach...teach...."

The class burst out laughing. Bulk's face turned bright red. But that was only the beginning.

The next scene was at the field the Power Rangers had cleaned up. Bulk stood in front of the mountain of trash bags. Again the picture was jerky, and Bulk's words were all chopped up. *"I pick...trash,"* he seemed to say.

When Bulk slipped on the banana peel and fell into the pile, even Ms. Appleby snickered.

Bulk was so upset that he

couldn't even speak! He just glared at Skull.

And then came the next scene. Bulk was smashing into a tower of aluminum cans at the youth center's recycling drive. His choppy edited video voice said, *"I...should be recycled."*

Kimberly was laughing so hard she was crying. Ms. Appleby's whole body shook as she tried not to giggle. In fact, only two people in the whole room weren't laughing.

Bulk, because he was so mad.

And Skull, because he was scared he was going to get creamed.

Finally Bulk exploded like a volcano. "I'M GONNA POUND YOU, CAMERAMAN!"

Skull jumped up out of his chair. The last thing the Power Rangers heard as Bulk chased Skull out of the room was, "I can fix it. I can fix it!"

Jason, Trini, Billy, Zack, and Kimberly grinned at one another. It had been a tough week. And a good week.

They were proud of their teamwork in cleaning up Angel Grove, and their teamwork in protecting the Earth from harm.

Best of all, it was great just to be hanging out again, having fun

in class together. As if they were
just ordinary kids.

Kids with a very big secret.